− WILDERNESS RIDGE −

W9-BTF-383

LURE of the LAKE

BY ART COULSON · ILLUSTRATED BY GREGOR FORSTER

STONE ARCH BOOKS
a capstone imprint

Published by Stone Arch Books, an imprint of Capstone.
1710 Roe Crest Drive
North Mankato, Minnesota 56003
capstonepub.com

Library of Congress Cataloging-in-Publication Data
Names: Coulson, Art, 1961– author. | Forster, Gregor, illustrator.
Title: Lure of the lake / by Art Coulson.
Description: North Mankato, Minnesota : Stone Arch Books, [2022] | Series:
Wilderness ridge | Audience: Ages 8–11 | Audience: Grades 4–6 | Summary: Twins
Harley and Rhiannon Hummingbird travel from their Oklahoma home to their
grandparents' new cabin in northern Wisconsin where they not only learn about
the best techniques in having a successful day fishing, but also about teamwork
and persistence.
Identifiers: LCCN 2021002842 (print) | LCCN 2021002843 (ebook) |
ISBN 9781663912312 (hardcover) | ISBN 9781663921963 (paperback) |
ISBN 9781663912282 (ebook pdf)
Subjects: CYAC: Fishing—Fiction. | Grandfathers—Fiction. | Twins—Fiction. |
Cooperativeness—Fiction. | Persistence—Fiction.
Classification: LCC PZ7.1.C6758 Lu 2022 (print) | LCC PZ7.1.C6758 (ebook) |
DDC [Fic]—dc23
LC record available at https://lccn.loc.gov/2021002842
LC ebook record available at https://lccn.loc.gov/2021002843

Editorial Credits
Editor: Alison Deering; Designer: Sarah Bennett; Media Researcher: Svetlana
Zhurkin; Production Specialist: Katy LaVigne

Design elements: Shutterstock: Mikhail Zyablov, SvartKat

For Cathy Coulson, who is still fishing somewhere.

Printed and bound in the USA.   4270

Table of Contents

CHAPTER ONE

At the Cabin

"Wow!" Harley said as we poured out of my grandparents' SUV and got our first look at their new cabin. It was huge, all wood and windows, with a covered front porch and a three-car garage.

For once, I didn't argue with my brother. *Wow is right*, I thought.

In my thirteen years, I had never seen a more beautiful lake house. And that was the best part—the lake. You could barely see all the way across. For the next two weeks, I'd be able to swim and fish right from the backyard.

This was definitely nicer than our apartment in Tulsa. But to be honest, at first I hadn't been excited about spending two weeks in the woods of Wisconsin. I'd wanted to spend the summer at home with my friends.

But then my parents had mentioned Grandma and Grandpa's new pontoon boat. They wanted to take us fishing on the lake every day.

I'd only been fishing a few times, but a boat sounded fun. Even if my baby brother had to tag along. Although we're technically twins, Harley was born twenty whole minutes after me. It was the next day, just after midnight, so we don't even share a birthday.

Most people can't even tell we're twins. For one thing, I'm a girl. And for another, we're *nothing* alike. Mom says it's like we came from different parents or something. More like different species.

"Like it?" Grandma asked. "It's your home away from home for the next two weeks, so let's get you settled in. There will be plenty of time to fish after supper."

Uncle Clayton, Mom's big brother, stepped out of the garage door and threw his arms open wide. Harley and I ran to him and gave him a big hug.

"Need some help?" he asked.

"I was thinking of showing the twins around the property before we head in," Grandpa said. "It's been a long ride." He turned to us. "How about it, you two? Want a little tour before we carry these bags in?"

He didn't have to ask twice. Harley and I ran toward the backyard. And there it was, tied to the dock—a big, white pontoon boat with blue striped seats and a blue top. The boat was huge! It even had a swimming platform and a sundeck.

I know where I'll be spending the next two weeks, I thought.

"Well, now that you've seen the outside, let's go in, get you settled, and have some supper," Grandma said. "I have some panfish to fry up, and I'll whip up some fry bread to go with it. Plus there are strawberry dumplings for dessert."

I smiled. Grandma and Grandpa had left the Cherokee Nation a long time ago for Grandpa's job as a biomedical researcher. But they hadn't forgotten how to make good food, just like back home in Oklahoma.

"Let's grab your bags," Grandpa said. "Then I can show you the garage. That's where we keep the fishing gear and the life jackets and such."

I grabbed my duffle and followed Grandpa to the garage. It was bigger than our whole apartment in Oklahoma!

Next to the backdoor, which led out to the lake, was a large brown cabinet. Inside were tackle boxes and nets and other fishing gear. Life jackets hung on wooden clothes hangers. On the side of the cabinet, a rod holder held a dozen fishing poles of various shapes and sizes.

Back in the main house, Grandpa said, "Let me show you to your rooms. Harley, you'll be in the spare bedroom. Rhiannon, we're going to put you in the big room downstairs. It'll be like having your own apartment."

I headed downstairs to start unpacking. Before long I smelled something magical— frying fish.

My stomach growled, and my mouth started to water. If had to guess, Grandma would also have a big pot of brown beans on the stove. A real taste of home—all the way up here in the north woods.

I ran up the stairs two at a time, but Harley had beaten me to the dining room table. He and Uncle Clay were already sitting there. Both of them had their napkins tucked into their shirt collars.

"Let's eat," Harley said. Uncle Clay just grinned.

Grandma and Grandpa brought the feast to the table, and we dug in.

After we had gobbled down our supper, Harley jumped up. "Let's go fishing!" he said. "I bet I catch way more fish than you do, Rhiannon."

"Wanna bet?" I said. I raced after my brother. I couldn't wait to get out on the lake.

CHAPTER TWO

The First Bite

We raced out to the garage and headed straight for the fishing rods.

"I want the blue one," Harley said.

I shrugged. "That's fine," I said. "The red one next to it is bigger and better for catching big bass." I had no idea if that last part was true, but I never missed the chance to give my brother a hard time.

Grandpa appeared in the garage a few minutes later. He grabbed a couple of life jackets out of the cabinet and handed them to us. Then he picked up his tackle box off the workbench.

"We've still got a few more hours of daylight left. Maybe we'll catch *tomorrow's* supper," Grandpa said.

Grandma came out too. She was carrying a big bag over her shoulder and a cooler. "Someone has to remember the bug spray and the refreshments," she said.

"Is Uncle Clay coming?" I asked.

"No, he usually takes a nap after supper. We'll probably hear him snoring all the way up the lake," Grandma said.

We got on the boat and settled in. Grandpa took his spot at the wheel. Grandma sat next to him. Harley and I plopped down in the swivel fishing chairs near the front of the boat.

As we boated up the lake, Harley and I hung on to the rails, watching the shoreline pass slowly by. When we passed people sitting by the water or roasting marshmallows over firepits, we waved. They all waved back.

Grandpa piloted the boat out to the middle of the lake and cut the engine. Grandma dropped an anchor off the front of the pontoon. Then they helped Harley and me get our rods set up for fishing.

"Let's use these little jigs and see what we can scare up," Grandpa said, taking the swivel at the end of my line. He attached what looked like a rainbow-colored half worm with blue feathers and a big hook coming out of its end.

"What's that supposed to be?" I asked him.

"That's called a crappie jig," Grandpa explained. "There are a lot of crappies in this lake. This time of the year, they like the cooler water here where it's a little deeper. They're real fighters and fun to catch."

"And good to eat," Grandma added. She was putting a similar jig on Harley's line. "We'll try these jigs for a while. And if they aren't biting, we might switch to some spinners."

"What's a spinner?" Harley asked.

Grandma reached into the top of the tackle box at her feet. She carefully pulled out a metal lure with colorful feathers.

"This is a spinner," she explained, holding the lure out so we could get a better look. "This shiny metal part spins as you reel it back through the water. It really gets the fish biting. When you're fishing, sometimes you have to keep trying different bait or lures to find what works."

Harley and I cast out a few times as our grandparents gave us pointers. After about twenty minutes, I felt a firm tug on my line.

Yes! I cheered silently. *My first fish!*

I wanted to dance with joy, but that feeling quickly turned to mild panic. I had no idea what to do next.

I held the rod tightly and turned to look at Grandpa. "Help?"

CHAPTER THREE

A Real Competition

"Set the hook," Grandpa said. He put his arms around me and gently gripped my arms. He pulled the rod tip up. "Now reel. You've got one!"

I reeled and pulled. The fish bent the rod and fought with all its might. Just when I thought I had the battle won, the fish gave a mighty tug. The line whizzed out of my reel.

"You're doing great, wesa. Keep at him," Grandpa said.

No one had called me wesa—the Cherokee word for "cat"—in a long time. Grandpa had called me that since I was a little girl.

He usually called Harley chooch, which is Cherokee for "boy." How basic.

I pulled and reeled for what seemed like hours, but was only a few minutes. My arms felt like they might fall off. Finally, I pulled in a pale yellow-and-white fish with black speckles on its side.

"That's a good one, wesa," Grandpa said. "That's a huge crappie. It must be almost a foot long. That's a keeper for sure."

Grandma lifted the top of something that looked like a built-in cooler.

"What's that?" I asked.

"This is a live well. It keeps the fish alive until we get them back to the cabin," she said. "Bring that fish over here so I can show you how to take it off the hook."

I did as I was told. Grandma reached right into the fish's mouth with her thumb and twisted out the hook with her other hand.

Once the fish was free, she dropped it into the bubbling water inside the live well. I went back to my lucky spot.

A moment later, Harley yelped and yanked at his rod. "Got one, got one, got one!"

His rod bent almost to the surface of the lake. Then, just as suddenly, it sprang back up.

"Looks like you lost him, chooch," Grandpa said. "But don't worry—there will be another. Let's reel in your line and check your jig. We need to make sure the fish didn't damage your lure or nip your line."

Once the jig passed Grandpa's inspection, Harley cast back out. I threw my jig out the other side.

Grandpa put a hand on Harley's shoulder. "You jerked a little hard on that last bite," he said. "When you hook the next one, pull up firmly but don't yank it. Set the hook and start reeling. That'll land you a big one."

Then we waited. I was learning pretty quickly that fishing was really a lot of waiting for something to happen. But when it did— *BAM!* It was the most fun anyone could have.

Harley yelped again. This time he pulled up on his rod to set the hook and started reeling.

"Good boy," Grandma said. "That's the way."

Before long, Harley swung a beautiful dark green and orange fish into the boat. It flopped on the deck.

"Nice," Grandpa said. "That's a sunfish and another keeper!"

"But not as big as mine," I said to Harley with a smirk. "I'm still winning."

"No, you're not," my brother snapped. "You only caught one. I hooked two."

"Only counts if you bring it onto the boat," I argued. "And my fish is bigger— I'm winning."

Grandpa held up his hands. "Okay, you two," he said. "If you're so competitive, I've got some good news for you. There's a huge youth bass tournament on our lake next weekend. First prize is a new rod and reel and a fully stocked tackle box. I say we get you two entered so you can put your competitive spirits to good use."

"Sign me up!" Harley said. "I'm going to win. And I'll have my own fishing rod and all the lures and hooks and sinkers I could ever want."

"Not so fast," I said. "You have to beat *me* to win. That won't happen."

Grandma laughed. "You two never let up," she said. "You're going to need a lot of practice fishing before the tournament. You'll be competing against kids who've been fishing this lake their whole lives. But I have good news for you—you can get up early tomorrow and fish the whole day if you want."

Normally getting up early—especially in the summer—just wasn't my thing. But if it meant beating my brother and proving I was the best fisherwoman, I'd be setting my alarm for six a.m.

CHAPTER FOUR

Practice Makes (Almost) Perfect

The next morning, Harley ate his bacon and eggs like some sort of rabid raccoon. He didn't even pause to breathe.

"Are you going to come up soon for air so we can make a plan?" I asked the raccoon masquerading as my brother.

"*Mmmmf*," he said. "What plan? We don't need a plan to go fishing. We dig some worms and head out on the dock."

I rolled my eyes. *Why do brothers make it so hard to make plans before rushing out to do something?*

"We need to come up with a plan for how we're going to catch some big bass today. We need to be ready for the tournament," I said.

"You guys planning to dig some worms?" Uncle Clay asked, putting down his magazine. "I can hook you up. I have a secret system. Ever heard of worm grunting?"

"Worms make noise?" Harley said.

Uncle Clay laughed like that was the funniest thing he'd ever heard. "No, worm grunting is a way to use sound to attract worms," he explained. "I'm going camping with my buddies in awhile, but I'll show you before I leave. It'll come in handy if you're planning to compete this weekend."

"You're going to need this," Grandma said, reaching into the pantry and pulling out an empty coffee can. She used a fork to poke some holes in the plastic lid. "Put some dirt in here—just a little. Then Uncle Clay can scare you up some night crawlers."

Uncle Clay took us out to his shed. He grabbed a pair of sticks cut from an old broom handle. One of the sticks had notches carved along its length.

Back outside, he knelt on the ground, jabbed the notched stick into the lawn, and began to run the other stick up and down the notches. It made a raspy, rattling sound.

"The vibrations travel down into the earth and call the worms to the surface," Uncle Clay said. He paused his "grunting" and moved the grass around with his free hand.

"I see one!" I said.

Uncle Clay popped the night crawler into the old coffee can Grandma had given us. After another twenty minutes of "grunting," we had a full bait bucket of fat worms.

"All right, you two should be all set," Uncle Clay said. "I'll expect a big fish fry when I get back from my camping trip."

"You bet! Thanks, Uncle Clay! Rhiannon, let's go catch some bass!" Harley said as he raced to the garage to grab a rod and reel.

Out at the end of the dock, we both cast our worms out toward the lily pads that floated all around us. Blue dragonflies darted around, landing on the lily pads and taking off again.

I was lost in my thoughts when . . .

"I got one!" Harley yelled. "It's a monster!"

He reeled in the smallest fish I'd ever seen.

"That's a bluegill," Grandpa said, walking onto the dock. "Better throw him back so he can get a little bigger. Be careful how you handle him. You don't want to hurt him. And be careful not to rub your hands on his body too much. He has a slime all around him that protects him in the water."

Harley frowned, but he unhooked the fish gently and placed it back in the lake. Just then, my rod bent toward the water.

"Now I've got one!" I shouted.

I pulled and reeled, but the fish didn't fight like my big crappie had the day before. I hoped it would be another keeper, but I wasn't sure. Was it a bass?

Finally the fish broke the surface of the water—another bluegill. But at least mine was bigger than Harley's.

"I'd throw him back too," Grandpa said. "There are bigger ones in there. Keep trying."

Over the next hour, Harley and I caught three more fish each, all sunfish and bluegills. A couple were keepers. But neither of us caught a single bass.

"There are no bass in this lake," Harley complained.

"Oh, but there are," Grandpa said. "Let me tell you about the fish the locals call 'the Beast'. . . ."

CHAPTER FIVE

A Real Fish Story

"The Beast, they say, is the size of a full-grown man," Grandpa said. "But it's a largemouth bass. It's the alpha predator in this lake. All the other fish fear it. Mothers won't let their toddlers wade into the lake when the Beast is near."

I scoffed. "Come on, Grandpa."

"I'm serious," he said. "Some people say the Beast has even leapt from the water and grabbed unsuspecting deer leaning down for a drink. It drags 'em in and swallows 'em whole!"

Harley's eyes got huge.

"A few years ago, an expert fisherman was taking part in a bass tournament on this very lake," Grandpa continued. "He had visions of catching the Beast and winning the grand prize."

"Did he do it?" Harley asked.

Grandpa nodded. "As luck would have it, he hooked the Beast. The big brute broke the surface of the water and danced across the lake on its massive tail. The fisherman said he figured the Beast had come to the surface just to look him in the eye before starting to fight."

"So what happened?" I asked. I had to admit, even I was intrigued by the story.

"The two of them fought for hours, man versus Beast. The fisherman pulled up on his rod with all of his might. He cranked the reel, drawing the fish toward his boat, inch by hard-fought inch." Grandpa paused. "Then the big fish made a run, pulling the fisherman—boat and all—up and down the length of the lake."

I stared out at the water, imagining the battle Grandpa was describing.

No fish is big enough to pull a boat across the lake, I thought. *Right?*

"Just when he thought he had the Beast tired out, the fisherman made a huge mistake," Grandpa said. "He let go of his rod with one hand to reach for his landing net. The Beast gave one massive pull and yanked the fisherman straight out of the boat and right into the lake. *Splash!*"

Across the water, someone jumped off their dock, echoing that *splash!* Harley and I both jumped a little.

"The fisherman swam for his life," Grandpa continued. "He'd lost his best rod and reel, but he made it back into his boat."

Harley and I both stared at Grandpa, spellbound. He looked back at us with a straight face.

"And somewhere to this day, the Beast uses that rod and reel to fish for unsuspecting anglers who are foolish enough to challenge him." He paused. "So, yes, there are bass in this lake. Big ones."

I looked over at Harley. My brother was staring at Grandpa with his eyes wide and his mouth hanging open.

I knew Grandpa's story was probably just that—a story. But still, there had to be *some* big bass in this lake. If not, they wouldn't hold the tournament here. And if the bass were there, I was going to catch them.

"Grandpa," I said. "Would you help us figure out how to catch some bass? Maybe even the Beast?"

Grandpa chuckled. "Talk to your Uncle Clay when he gets back from camping. He can tell you the best lures to use to catch a lunker," he said. "Your uncle is the real bass fisherman in the family. I'm just the storyteller."

CHAPTER SIX

A Better Bass Trap

Three long days later, Uncle Clay drove his old truck down the driveway and parked in front of the garage. As he unpacked his camping gear and started to pile it in the garage, Harley and I surrounded him.

"Uncle Clay, will you show us your bass lures?" Harley asked.

"We need to know how to catch bass if I'm going to win the tournament," I added.

"Whoa, whoa, hold on, you two. Give a fellow some room," Uncle Clay said. "Let me finish stowing my gear, and I'll give you both a bass-fishing lesson."

We waited by the workbench in the garage until Uncle Clay came back in with his big tackle box. He opened the top and folded out three levels of compartments.

Each compartment held a lure. Some were shaped a little like fish, though they were all sorts of colors. Others looked like worms. Still others were just shiny bits of metal with hooks dangling from them.

Uncle Clay pulled out a big, green plastic lure. "What do you think this is?" he asked, holding it out so Harley and I could look at it more closely.

"Looks like a frog," Harley said.

"Right you are, sport," Uncle Clay said. "A frog. And bass *love* them. I've caught so many bass with this frog that I'm beginning to think it might be magic."

He winked at us, but I wasn't entirely sure he was kidding.

Uncle Clay reached back into the tackle box. He pulled out a fat, gray lure with a thin tail and a set of three hooks hanging off it.

"And this?" he asked.

"Not a frog," Harley said, stating the obvious.

"Looks like a mouse," I said.

"Yes, indeed—a mousie," Uncle Clay said. "Something else a bass will hop right into your boat for." He put the mouse back, then walked over to the rack of fishing rods by the door. "Now who wants to catch some bass?"

As we ran out onto the dock, Grandpa and Grandma walked across the lawn carrying folding chairs and rods of their own.

"Some of the best fishing is right off our dock," Grandpa said, setting down his chair. "I think I'll give our boat a rest today and fish right here."

Uncle Clay helped us put some lures on our rods. Harley chose the frog, and I chose the mouse. He showed us how to cast the lure in an arc and onto a lily pad. Then he pulled it back gently so that it dropped into the water.

"That gets their attention," Uncle Clay said. "It's like a real frog or mouse hopping off the lily pad into the water. The bass like to hide under branches, overhangs, and even lily pads. Easier to surprise their prey that way."

I did exactly what Uncle Clay said, but it didn't work for me. I didn't even get a nibble. Neither did Harley.

Grandpa was fishing with what looked like a black lizard. It had a yellow head and yellow feet. In front of its head was a small metal spinning thing.

"What's that?" I asked.

"I rigged up a spinner to a salamander," Grandpa said. "I've had a lot of luck fishing here in our little cove with this sort of rig. But today it doesn't seem to be attracting the fish."

Grandma had a rainbow-colored plastic fish on her line. It rattled when she shook it.

"It's a rattler," she explained. "Bass can hear it from miles away. They come running like it's their dinner bell."

We all cast out our lines and reeled them in over and over again. Harley and I changed lures a million times, trying different ways to catch a bass. Nothing seemed to be working. We fished from mid-morning to early afternoon without even one nibble.

Grandpa reeled in his line. "Well, everyone, what do you say we go inside and grab a sandwich? We can try our luck again a little later."

"You all go on ahead," Grandma said.

"Aren't you coming?" Grandpa said.

"Just one more cast," she said. "I'll be in after that."

Inside, Grandpa served up his specialty: peanut-butter-and-jelly sandwiches and green grapes. We all stood around the island in the kitchen, eating.

Then, *bang!* The screen door slammed shut.

We all turned to look. Grandma stood there with a big grin on her face and an even bigger bass in her right hand.

"Grandma!" I exclaimed. "How did you catch that bass?"

"Persistence," she said. "That's the most important tool in any angler's tackle box."

CHAPTER SEVEN

Catch and Release

First thing Wednesday morning, Harley and I ran up to the tackle shop to enter the tournament. Grandpa came with us and helped us fill out the forms. Then we turned them in to the owner, who wrote our names on a big board behind the counter. There were already lots of other names listed there.

When we got back to the lake house, we took a picnic lunch out on the pontoon. The rest of the day was spent fishing with Grandma, Grandpa, and Uncle Clay. Grandpa was right—Uncle Clay was a bass champion.

"Whoa! Got one," Uncle Clay said as he reeled in the largest bass I'd seen all week. "Smallmouth, nice size."

"How'd you do that?" I asked.

Uncle Clay grinned. "Caught him with my mousie. Told you they loved them!" He took the fish off the hook, then leaned over the rail and gently released it back into the water.

"Hey! What are you doing?" Harley said. "That was a monster fish."

Uncle Clay smiled and cast his mousie back toward the weeds. "I let him go so he'll be here for you guys to catch this weekend. Besides, I don't feel like cleaning fish today."

Grandpa and Grandma laughed.

I didn't have time to join in the laughter because just then something big hit my popper. *Splash!* A huge bass jumped out of the water and twisted in the sun before splashing back into the lake.

"Reel, girl, reel! You've got her," Grandma said.

I pulled and cranked and finally got the fish into the boat. It wasn't as big as Uncle Clay's, but I was still proud.

"You can keep her if you want," Uncle Clay said. "I'll even clean her for you."

I took the fish off the line and held it up so Harley could snap my picture with his phone. Then I walked over to the rail and lowered the bass back into the water.

"I think I'll wait to catch her again this weekend when it counts," I said.

Harley reeled in his line, then walked over to where Grandpa sat by the steering wheel. "Will you teach me to drive the pontoon so I can be the captain this weekend?" he asked.

Grandpa shook his head. "Sorry, chooch. There'll be a lot of boats out on the lake. You kids can use the canoe for the tournament."

Harley groaned, but Grandpa added, "That way you'll be able to paddle into some of the smaller coves and inlets where the bass are hanging out this time of the year."

Harley nodded and walked back over to the rail. He leaned down to pick another spinner out of the tackle box. This one was a huge rig with bright-green, rubbery fringe and a large metal spinning fin. He attached it to his line and cast it out toward a cluster of lily pads.

Screeeeeeeee! Harley jumped. A bass hit his lure and began running out his line as it swam away from our boat.

"Set it, Harley, then reel him in," Grandma said.

Harley landed a really nice smallmouth— maybe even bigger than the one I'd caught and released. I wasn't going to tell him that, though.

Harley walked over and put his fish in the live well. "I'll catch another one on Saturday," he said. "I'm eating this one."

* * *

The next morning, Grandpa loaded up the canoe and gave us a quick lesson on how to paddle and steer. He watched us as Harley and I paddled around the cove by the dock.

Mostly we spun in place and fought to find a rhythm so we could paddle smoothly in the same direction. But at least we didn't capsize.

"Tomorrow, I think you should take your fishing gear out and practice casting from the canoe," Grandma said when we broke for lunch. "That way you'll be all ready to hit the water safely on Saturday."

I nodded. After another day of canoe practice, with a little fishing thrown in, it would *finally* be Saturday—tournament day.

CHAPTER EIGHT

The Big Day

I was feeling confident as we headed to the bait shop at the end of the lake to sign in for the tournament. We'd caught a lot of bass over the past few days. The lessons from Uncle Clay and the variety of lures in Grandpa's tackle box had really helped.

"You can fish until two o'clock," the bait shop owner told us. "Remember, bring your five biggest fish to the weigh-in. No scrawny ones." She winked at Grandpa and chuckled. "We'll write everyone's totals on the board behind me so everyone can see what great fishermen and fisherwomen you all are."

When we got back to the cabin, Harley and I headed for the dock. Grandpa had already set up the canoe for us. There was a rod and reel, a full tackle box, and a life jacket for each of us.

Harley and I stepped down into the canoe. My brother sat on a little bench near the front. I sat on one at the back.

"Why don't you plan to get back to the dock at one o'clock?" Grandpa suggested. "That way we'll have plenty of time to get stuff put away before we head to the bait shop and weigh all those fish. Good luck!"

Harley and I each picked up a paddle and started to push away from the dock. It was hard to paddle with our bulky life jackets on. We made slow progress up the lake.

Finally, we made it to a nice spot where a fallen tree hung out over the water. Three turtles sunned themselves on the trunk.

"Let's stop here and try our luck," I said as I put down my paddle.

"No, let's go out to the middle," Harley argued. "That's where the big ones are." He paddled by himself, which made the canoe spin in circles. "Come on, Rhi. Help me."

I crossed my arms and glared at him. "This spot looks really good. Remember what Uncle Clay said?" I pointed to the tree. "Bass like that sort of hiding place."

Harley returned my glare. "Fine. We'll fish here for a few minutes, then we'll paddle out to the middle and catch some big ones."

I put a spinner on my line. Uncle Clay had said it was a rooster tail, which was a funny name for a lure. I cast toward the fallen tree. Harley used a rattler and cast near where my spinner had landed.

"Hey! Don't get tangled with my line," I told him.

"You're not my boss," he said. "Just fish and mind your own business."

We each cast six or seven times but didn't even get a bite. I put my rod down and picked up my paddle.

"What are you waiting for?" I said. "Let's go out to the middle, out by those weeds."

By the time we got out to the middle, it was almost eleven-thirty. We had spent almost two hours arguing. There wasn't much time left.

And we still don't have a single fish, I thought, feeling frustrated.

We had done so well in the days leading up to the tournament. And today we were getting skunked.

"We can only spend about an hour out here. Then we have to head back to the dock," I said. "We need to get serious if we're going to win this tournament."

But things didn't get better. In the last hour, we caught a couple of crappies, a sunfish, and the weeds on the bottom. That last one was Harley. He yanked and tugged. Finally, he broke his line.

"That was my best rattler," he said. "That's it. I quit. We've been out here for three hours, and all we've caught are small panfish. Not one bass."

"Whose fault is that?" I snapped. But my heart just wasn't in it. I was disappointed too. "Let's paddle back to the dock and tell Grandpa the bad news."

* * *

Grandpa made us go to the weigh-in anyway. He said we needed to be good sports and cheer on the other kids. The winner was a local girl. She'd caught five bass weighing a total of 17.6 pounds. Even I was impressed.

We spent the rest of the day Saturday swimming in the lake. The weather was great, but I couldn't shake my disappointment.

That evening, I excused myself right after supper. "I think I'll go in and read for a bit," I said. "I'm pretty tired from all the paddling and swimming."

I couldn't wait to go to bed and forget about my rotten day.

CHAPTER NINE

The Beast

The next morning, Harley and I ate in silence. "So, what's the plan for today?" Uncle Clay asked.

I poked at my cereal and didn't look up. Harley just shrugged.

"Oh, come on, you two. If I sat around and moped every time I got skunked while bass fishing, I'd never get to go out on the water again," Uncle Clay said. "You head home at the end of this week. This might be your last chance to catch the Beast."

I looked up at my brother. He returned my stare.

"Want to?" I asked him.

Harley shrugged again, but he looked interested. "I guess so," he said.

We grabbed our gear and piled in the canoe. Then we pushed off from the dock and started to paddle. But every time I tried to steer us one way, Harley paddled in the opposite direction.

"Harley!"

"Rhiannon!"

Grrr. I was getting so tired of this.

"Fine, we can just sit here and spin in the water," I told him.

"Fine," he said.

We sat like that for several minutes, watching the occasional fish jump out of the water. I looked across the lake and saw a pair of kids about our age paddling a canoe down the shoreline.

Their arms and shoulders seemed to move together like a machine as they lifted and plunged their paddles. The canoe glided noiselessly along.

Then I heard the girl in the front of the canoe laugh. The boy said something in reply, but I couldn't hear him. I could see his big smile, though. They were having all kinds of fun, not wasting time fighting and arguing.

Why can't that be us? I thought. I took a deep breath. Maybe it could be.

"Harley? Want to try again?" I said. I could see he was watching the two kids paddling down the lake too.

"Yeah, Rhi. We can do this. Maybe if we work together we can get where we're going a lot faster," he said. "Then we'll have more time for fishing."

"Harley Hummingbird, you are a genius," I said. "So where should we paddle first?"

"How about that tree that fell in the water, the one we fished by during the tournament?" my brother suggested. "There are bound to be some big ones in there."

We paddled smoothly toward our spot, trying to keep our strokes in sync. I hummed a song so that we could find a steady rhythm.

For the rest of the afternoon, we fished. We didn't even stop for lunch. I had two granola bars in my bag, so I shared one with my brother.

By the time we paddled back into the dock, we had a stringer full of fish—sunfish, bluegills, perch, and even a few bass.

But the Beast had eluded us.

"That's okay, sis," Harley said. "We'll get him tomorrow. We're getting pretty good at this."

"Her," I corrected. "We'll get *her* tomorrow. Who said the Beast was a boy?"

CHAPTER TEN

One More Cast

The final three days of our vacation seemed to fly by. Harley and I fished every day, sometimes from the dock, sometimes from the pontoon. We caught a lot of fish, and we ate most of them.

But we didn't hook the Beast—never even saw her swim by.

On our final day there, Grandpa said he wanted to take us on one last pontoon ride. Harley and I eagerly agreed. Our flight back to Tulsa didn't leave until the evening, so we had most of the day to hang out at the lake.

While we fished, Harley and I swapped stories about all of the fish we had caught over the past two weeks. We had both gotten better at matching our lures and our fishing techniques to the conditions.

After a few hours on the water, Grandma said, "Well, it's just about time to head in and get some lunch. We'll finish packing your bags and get them in the car. If we get to the airport a little early, that's okay. Better early than late."

"Pull your lines in," Grandpa said. He started the engine and headed for the dock.

I reached in the tackle box near my feet and pulled out Uncle Clay's mouse lure. I snapped it to my swivel. I stood at the rail and threw the mouse as far as I could toward the weeds along the shore.

"One more cast," I said, smiling at Grandma. "I wanted to use some of that persistence you were telling us about."

Just then my rod jerked, almost flying out of my hands. Harley had to put his arms around my waist to keep me from tumbling over the rail.

Grandpa quickly cut the engine. I pulled back on the rod to set the hook and started reeling.

The fish jumped and seemed to dance across the lake toward us. It was the biggest bass I had ever seen.

The bass danced and splashed, putting on a show before diving back into the lake. My rod bent even more toward the water.

"The Beast!" Grandpa said, clapping his hands. Uncle Clay danced a little jig.

"You've got her, Rhi. Stay steady," Grandma said. "That's my girl."

The Beast and I fought for almost fifteen minutes. My arms burned from the constant tugging and reeling.

I finally had her almost to the side of the boat. Uncle Clay unhooked a long-handled net from just below the railing.

And then my heart sank. In an instant I went from fighting with all my might to holding a rod with nothing on the other end. The Beast had thrown the hook.

I watched her swim away. I had tears in my eyes.

Grandma said, "It's okay, Rhi. You were the only one to hook the Beast this summer. That makes you a champion angler in anyone's book."

I laid my rod down on the bench and closed my tackle box, trying not to cry. I felt a hand on my shoulder from behind.

"It's okay, sis," Harley said. "Better you didn't catch the Beast today. That way she'll be here next summer when we come back to visit."

I turned around and hugged him. When had my brother gotten so wise?

Harley was right. There was always next year.

And next year, the Beast was mine.

About the Author

photo by Ivy Vainio

Art Coulson, Cherokee, was an award-winning journalist and the first executive director of the Wilma Mankiller Foundation in Oklahoma. He grew up fishing and crabbing most weekends with his family, especially his mother who was an avid angler. His first children's book, *The Creator's Game: A Story of Baaga'adowe/Lacrosse* (Minnesota Historical Society Press, 2013), told of the deep spiritual and cultural connections of American Indian people to the sport of lacrosse. Art still plays traditional Cherokee stickball, an original version of lacrosse, when he is visiting friends and family in the Cherokee Nation of Oklahoma. Art lives in Apple Valley, Minnesota.

About the Illustrator

photo by Gregor Forster

Gregor Forster studied scientific illustration at the Zurich University of Arts in Switzerland. After finishing his studies in 2015, he started illustrating fiction and nonfiction picture books, educational books, and advertisements. When illustrating children's books, Gregor loves to research new topics and learn about the world the story takes place in. He loves to entertain, educate, and amaze children as much as adults with his illustrations. When Gregor isn't drawing or painting, he might be free diving somewhere in cold Swiss lakes.

Glossary

alpha (AL-fuh)—having the most power in a group of animals or people

angler (ANG-glur)—a person who fishes

capsize (KAP-syz)— to tip over in the water

jig (JIG)—a lure that is jerked up and down while fishing; jigs usually look like insects

live well (LIVE WEL)—a well for keeping fish alive in a fishing boat by allowing water to circulate through it

lure (LOOR)—a fake bait used in fishing

persistence (per-SIS-tuhns)—the act of continually trying to do something

pontoon (pon-TOON)—a flat-bottomed boat; also a float that helps a boat or vehicle stay above water

predator (PRED-uh-tur)—an animal that hunts other animals for food

prey (PRAY)—an animal hunted by another animal for food

spinner (SPIN-er)—a small device that spins and that is used by fishermen and fisherwomen to attract fish

tournament (TUR-nuh-muhnt)—a series of contests between several people or teams ending in one winner

Talk About It

1. Uncle Clay, Grandma, and Grandpa offer the twins many tips and tricks for catching bass. Which did you find the most interesting or useful? Talk about why.

2. On one of the family's outings, Uncle Clay and Rhiannon practice catch-and-release fishing. What are some reasons an angler might release his or her catch? Talk about what you would have done in that situation.

3. Learning a new hobby can be a challenge. There are new skills to master and even new vocabulary to learn. Have you ever started a new hobby? What were some of the challenges? Talk about it.

Write About It

1. Rhiannon and Harley are unsuccessful in the big bass tournament because they don't work as a team. Write a paragraph about a time you worked with another person or a team. Did you succeed in what you were trying to do? Why or why not?

2. What are some of the ways that anglers fish for bass? Look back through the story. Write a list of tips you learned.

3. Have you ever been fishing yourself? Write about one of your favorite fishing memories. (If you haven't been, imagine the perfect fishing trip.) What made (or would make) that fishing trip memorable?

More About Fishing

Fishing is one of the most popular outdoor activities. According to the Outdoor Foundation and Recreational Boating & Fishing Foundation, close to 50 million people fish each year. In the United States, almost one-quarter of all children went fishing at least once in the past year. The average angler went fishing eighteen times last year—that's more than once a month.

Fishing is something people have done for fun, to feed their families, and to make a living for hundreds of thousands of years. Archaeologists have found evidence that Neanderthals fished for their food more than 200,000 years ago.

The equipment needed for fishing is simple— a pole, fishing line, and a hook. Depending on location and what kind of fish they hope to catch, anglers also use sinkers, bobbers, leaders, swivels, and other tackle. Different baits and lures are used to attract different kinds of fish.

There are almost as many ways to fish as there are types of fish. Some people fish using large nets. Spearfishing and gigging involve using a long, sharp fork to spear fish. Noodling requires a person to reach into the water and catch fish with his or her hands. In some places where rivers and lakes freeze in the winter, people fish by cutting holes in the ice and dropping in a line.

Fishing is managed by state and tribal governments, which issue licenses or permits to anglers. Some fishing may be done year-round, while fishing for other species is limited to certain times or seasons. To find the rules and seasons for your area, look up the natural resources department for your state or tribe.

Check Out All the
Wilderness Ridge Titles

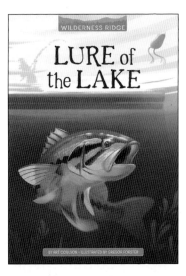

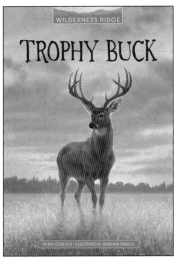

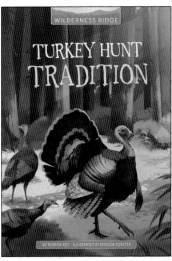